A CHILDREN'S PROBLEM SOLVING BOOK

Mommy, Don't Go

Written by Elizabeth Crary   Illustrated by Marina Megale

Parenting Press, Inc.
SEATTLE, WASHINGTON

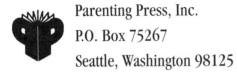

Parenting Press, Inc.
P.O. Box 75267
Seattle, Washington 98125

Ways to teach children how to solve social problems are thoroughly explained in Problem-Solving Techniques in Childrearing *by Myrna B. Shure and George Spivack, San Francisco: Jossey-Bass Publishers, 1978.*

Book design by Elizabeth Watson
Formatting by Margarite D. Hargrave

Library of Congress Cataloging-in-Publication Data
Crary, Elizabeth, 1942-
      Mommy, don't go / by Elizabeth Crary ; illustrated by Marina Megale. -- 2nd ed.
          p.   cm. -- (A children's problem solving book)
      Summary: Illustrates the use of problem-solving skills, critical thinking, and conflict resolution through an example of mother-child separation.
        ISBN 1-884734-20-0 (pbk.). -- ISBN 1-884734-21-9 (lib. bdg.)
        1. Mother and child--Juvenile literature.   2. Separation anxiety in children--Juvenile literature.   [1. Mother and child.   2. Separation anxiety.   3. Literary recreations.]   I. Megale, Marina, ill.   II. Title.   III. Series: Crary, Elizabeth, 1942-   Children's problem solving book.
HQ755.85.C73   1996
306.874'3--dc20   96-23352
                                                                           CIP

Parents (and Others) Can Teach Children How to Think

I wrote the six *Children's Problem Solving Books* to help children learn to solve social problems. Each book explores a common problem for children: sharing, waiting, wanting, being lost, and name calling. These books are interactive, and children have fun thinking about the questions. Your young listener/reader will enjoy helping the children in the stories decide what to do to solve their problems.

Why These Books Look Different

These books look different because they do something different. They teach children to think about the problems they face. These books help in three ways. First, they model a process for thinking before acting. Second, they offer children several different ways to handle each situation. Third, they show children how one person's behavior affects other people. Research shows that the more ideas a child has to solve social problems, the better his or her social adjustment is.

How to Use These Books

You will find questions to ask your child on almost every page. Before you read the *italic* words, give your child time to think about the question and answer it her- or himself. Each time a CHOICE (in the gray box) is offered, let her or him choose what to do. Turn to the page selected to see what happens. There are no "right" or "wrong" answers. All alternatives teach children to think. The outcomes of each allow children to discover for themselves why some actions are more effective than others.

I have included questions about feelings to encourage children to think about how they and others feel when there is a problem. Children need to know that feelings are not "good" or "bad," they just are. Awareness of feelings helps children think of solutions that meet their own and other's needs.

Transition from Story to Real Life

The last page of each book invites readers to list their own ideas about other ways to solve the story child's problem. With guidance your child can use the techniques learned in the book to think of ways to solve problems he or she has. For children who are reluctant to talk about solutions to their personal problems, you can ask them what the character in the book might do in a situation similar to theirs.

Through reading these books you are helping your child learn how to make good decisions. Further, you are teaching her or him that thinking and learning are fun. Children learn to think by thinking, not by being told what to do. Give your child many opportunities to practice thinking and problem solving. Have fun!

Elizabeth Crary
Seattle, Washington

This is a story about Matthew.

He likes to climb trees, race cars with a friend, and help his mother cook.

Usually Matthew has lots of fun. But right now he is upset because his mother is going on a trip.

Marta, the babysitter, will come and stay with him, but he wants his mother to stay home.

What can Matthew do so he will feel better?

(Wait for child to respond after each question. Look at page 3, "How to Use These Books," for ways to encourage children to think for themselves.)

CHOICES

Matthew can think of nine things to do. He can—

What will he try first?

(Wait for child to respond. Then turn to the appropriate page and continue the story.)

6

Try to make his mother stay home

Matthew decides to try to make his mother stay home.

He locks the door. He wraps his arms around her legs and won't let go. He cries, "Mommy, don't go! Mommy, don't go!"

She says, "I know you don't want me to go, Matt. And I still need to go."

Matthew clings tighter.

Mom asks him, "Do you want to let go and wave goodbye to me, or shall I ask Marta to hold you while I leave?"

Matthew decides to let go.

How does Matthew feel?

Sad and mad. Sad that she is still going. Mad because he could not make her stay home.

CHOICES

What do you think Matthew will do next?

Pretend he doesn't care . . . . *page 16*

Cry . . . . *page 18*

Ask his mother to stay home

Matthew decides to ask his mother to stay. He tells her how he feels, "Mommy, don't go. I don't want you to go. I'll miss you."

"I'll miss you, too, Matt. You are very special to me. Is there something particular you are worried about?" his mother asks.

"I'm worried you'll get hurt and die or something," Matt sobs.

Mother sits down beside Matthew and replies, "That idea is very scary. Is there something I could do to help you feel less scared?"

"I don't know. I can't think of anything," he says.

"Do you want me to think of some ideas?" his mother asks.

"Yes," Matthew answers promptly.

(Turn to page 12.)

10

Mother thinks a bit and says, "Well, I can think of three things that
    might help.
    "I could let you keep something special of mine until I get home.
    "I could call you while I'm gone, to let you know I'm fine.
    "We could see if your very good friend could visit while I'm gone."
"Do those ideas help?" Mom asks.
"Yes," Matthew replies. "I want something to keep until you get back."

How does Matthew feel now?
    *Glad and a little sad. Glad that he is important to his mom. And a
    little sad because she is still going.*

(Turn to page 14.)

Keep something special of Mom's

Matthew is worried that his mom will not come back. "Mommy, can I have something of yours?" Matthew asks.

"Will it help you feel better if you have something of mine?" asks Mom.

"Yes," Matt replies. "Then I can touch it whenever I want to."

Mother answers, "You are more important to me than my things are. And, yes, you may keep something of mine until I get back."

"Here are three ideas—

"You could pick a piece of jewelry from my jewelry box.

"You could hold my fuzzy robe, and snuggle up with it if you feel lonely.

"You can keep a picture of me to look at until I get home."

"Hmm … I want the pretty cat necklace," says Matthew.

"Okay," Mom smiles. "Bring me my jewelry box."

How does Matthew feel?

Happy. He has a special thing to hold until Mom comes home.

How do you like this ending?

(If you want to continue, turn to page 26.)

Pretend he doesn't care

Matthew is very mad his mother is going. He decides to try to make her feel bad. He pretends he doesn't care she is going.

He gets his cars and races them around in the middle of the living room. He doesn't look at his mother, even when she puts her coat on.

When she says, "I'm ready to go now," he pretends he doesn't hear.

Mother asks, "Do you want a hug before I go?" Matt says nothing.

Mother blows him a kiss and says, "Make your day go the way you want it to. I love you even when I am gone."

How does Matthew feel?

Terrible. He tried to make his mother feel bad, but it didn't work. And he didn't get his goodbye hug.

CHOICES
What will Matthew do now?
Tell the babysitter he is sad . . . . *page 20*
Make a surprise for his mom . . . . *page 22*

Cry

Matthew starts to cry. He sits on the sofa and cries, and cries, and cries.

While Matthew cries his mother gets ready to go. When she is finished she comes to Matthew and says, "I love you when I am here and I love you when I am gone. Remember, Mommy always comes back. If you need help thinking of ways to cheer up, you can ask for help."

Then she gives Matthew a hug and leaves.

How does Matthew feel now?

Mad and sad and glad. Mad that crying didn't make his mother stay. Sad because she has gone. Glad that she will come back.

CHOICES
What do you think Matthew will do next?
Tell the babysitter he is sad . . . . *page 20*
Cheer himself up . . . . *page 24*

Tell the babysitter he is sad

Matthew decides to tell Marta he is unhappy.

He finds Marta in the kitchen making coffee. "Marta, I wish Mommy didn't go. I want her back now!"

Marta says, "You love your mother and you miss her. Your mother loves you, too. Do you want to be sad the whole time she is gone?"

Matthew decides he doesn't. "No!" he replies.

"Okay. Can you think of some ways to be happy while she is gone?" she asks.

"Yes! I could make a surprise for Mom, or cuddle up and read a story."

How does Matthew feel?

Happy. He knows his mom loves him even though she is gone. And he has thought of some things he wants to do.

CHOICES

What will Matthew do now?

Make a surprise for his mom . . . . *page 22*
Read a story. . . . . *page 26*

20

Make a surprise for his mom

Matthew wants to feel better. He decides to do something special for his mom while she is gone. He wants to make a surprise to give her when she gets back.

He and Marta talk about what he can do. Since Matthew likes to cook, they decide to make a batch of welcome back cookies for his mother.

How does Matthew feel now?

Happy. He did feel sad. Now that he is working on a surprise, he feels happy.

How do you like this ending?

Cheer himself up

Matthew's mother has gone. He is feeling very sad and decides to make
   himself feel better.
He thinks of several things he can do—
   Cuddle up in the rocking chair with his mother's fuzzy robe.
   Pet Midnight, his cat.
   Ask Marta, the babysitter, for a hug.

What do you think he will do?

(Turn to page 28.)

Ask for a hug

Mother has gone now. Matthew feels very lonely. He would like to feel better but he is not sure how. Suddenly he remembers his mom said that if he needs loving, he can ask Marta for a hug.

He runs to find Marta. He says, "Marta, I feel sad because my mommy is gone. Will you give me a hug?"

"Sure!" Marta replies. "You don't have to feel sad to get a hug. You can have one anytime."

Marta gives Matt a big hug, then asks, "Is there anything special you want?"

Matt thinks for a moment and says, "Yes, I want a story."

"Okay," agrees Marta, "you pick it out."

How does Matthew feel?

Sad and glad. Sad that his mommy is gone. Glad because he can still get loving.

How do you like this ending?

Matthew decides to cuddle up with his mother's robe. He gets the robe and climbs into the rocking chair.

The robe feels warm and cozy. Rocking is almost as nice as being with his mother. Soon he does not feel quite so lonely and worried.

He gets his favorite book to look at while he rocks. He pretends his mom is reading to him.

How does Matthew feel?

Better. He still misses his mother, but he now has found a way to feel good and cozy.

How do you like this ending?

Idea page

Here is a list of Matthew's ideas.

Start your own list of things you can do when your mommy or daddy is going away. Add more ideas as you think of them.

Matthew's ideas

✓ Try to make his mother stay home
✓ Ask his mother to stay home
✓ Tell his mother how he feels
✓ Keep something special of Mom's
✓ Pretend he doesn't care
✓ Cry
✓ Tell the babysitter he is sad
✓ Make a surprise for his mom
✓ Play with his cat
✓ Ask for a hug
✓ Ask for a story
✓ Cuddle with his mom's fuzzy robe
✓ Rock in the rocking chair

Your ideas

Solving social problems ...

Children's Problem Solving Books teach children to think about their problems. Each interactive story allows the reader to choose the main character's actions and see what happens as a result. Useful with 3–8 years. 32 pages, illustrated. $6.95 each. Written by Elizabeth Crary, illustrated by Marina Megale.

See next page for ordering information, please.

Megan and Amy want to play with the same truck.
ISBN 1-884734-14-6, paper

Danny is tired of playing alone and wants to share friends.
ISBN 1-884734-18-9, paper

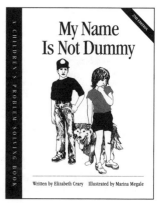

Jenny doesn't like being called "dummy."
ISBN 1-884734-16-2, paper

Gabriela has lost her dad at the zoo and is unhappy.
ISBN 1-884734-24-3, paper

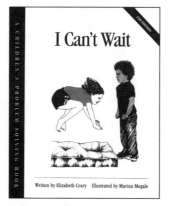

Luke wants his turn jumping on the mattress NOW!
ISBN 1-884734-22-7, paper

Matthew doesn't want to stay with the babysitter.
ISBN 1-884734-20-0, paper

Library-bound editions available. Call Parenting Press, Inc. at **1-800-992-6657** for information.

Prices subject to change without notice.

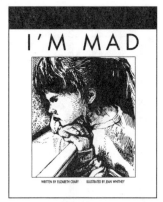

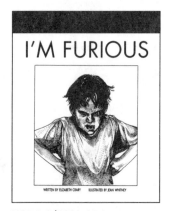